This book belongs to:

_____

GROSSET & DUNLAP
Published by the Penguin Group
Penguin Group (USA) LLC, 375 Hudson Street, New York, New York 10014, USA

USA | Canada | UK | Ireland | Australia | New Zealand | India | South Africa | China

penguin.com
A Penguin Random House Company

The stories in this book were originally published individually as *A Berry Bitty Christmas* in 2012, *The Snow Dance* and *My First Sleepover* in 2010, *Meet Cherry Jam!* in 2012, *Gymnastics Fun* in 2014, and *A Berry Bitty Ballet* in 2013.

Strawberry Shortcake™ and related trademarks © 2014 Those Characters From Cleveland, Inc. Used under license by Penguin Young Readers Group. All rights reserved. Published by Grosset & Dunlap, a division of Penguin Young Readers Group, 345 Hudson Street, New York, New York 10014. GROSSET & DUNLAP is a trademark of Penguin Group (USA) LLC. Manufactured in China.

ISBN 978-0-448-48360-3   10 9 8 7 6 5 4 3 2 1

Berry Merry Holiday
TREASURY

Grosset & Dunlap
An Imprint of Penguin Group (USA) LLC

TABLE OF CONTENTS

A Berry Bitty Christmas

By Amy Ackelsberg

Illustrated by Laura Thomas

It was Christmastime in Berry Bitty City! Strawberry Shortcake, Lemon Meringue, and Raspberry Torte were taking a walk through town to see how their friends were getting ready for the holiday.

13

"Don't you just love this time of year?" asked Strawberry as they watched Orange Blossom and Plum Pudding hang decorations.
"I love all the twinkling lights," exclaimed Lemon.

14

"I love all the music!" said Raspberry as they listened to Cherry Jam and Blueberry Muffin rehearse Christmas carols.

"We should do something to make this year extra special," said Lemon.

"Yes!" agreed Raspberry.

"Hmm . . . ," said Strawberry as she watched Postmaster
Bumblebee deliver holiday packages.

"I know!" said Strawberry. "Let's exchange gifts! We'll draw names and then get a present for the friend whose name we choose. But don't tell anyone who you picked. That way, each gift will be a berry special and unique surprise!"

"What a great idea!" everyone agreed.

Later, over lunch at Strawberry's café, Lemon wrote down each girl's name and put them in Strawberry's hat. Everyone took turns choosing a name.

When Strawberry reached into the hat, she drew Blueberry's name, and when
Blueberry's turn came . . .

19

Blueberry drew Strawberry's name!

After they finished eating, the girls went home to plan their gifts.

All the next day, Strawberry tried hard to think of the perfect present for Blueberry. "Blueberry is one of my berry best friends," Strawberry told Pupcake and Custard. "I want to give her something fruitastic!"

Meanwhile, Blueberry knew exactly what to give Strawberry. She hurried to Raspberry's boutique.

At the boutique, Blueberry found the sparkly berry charm that Strawberry had been wanting for her charm bracelet.

When Strawberry sees my gift, she'll know how important she is to me, thought Blueberry.

"I'd like to trade this for the charm," said Blueberry as she handed something to Raspberry.

"Blueberry, isn't that your favorite pen?" cried Raspberry.

"It is," Blueberry replied. "I love my pen, but I know someone who will love this charm even more."

It was almost Christmas, and Strawberry still had no idea what to give Blueberry. Then she spotted a pretty journal at Orange's store.

This is perfect for Blueberry! thought Strawberry. *She can write in it with her favorite pen!*

"I'd like to trade my charm bracelet for this journal," Strawberry told Orange.
"But, Strawberry, you love that bracelet!" exclaimed Orange. "Are you sure?"
"I'm sure," replied Strawberry. "This journal will make a great friend berry happy."

The next day was Christmas! The girls gathered at Plum's dance studio to open presents.

Plum went first. "A new dance outfit!" she cried. "Thank you, Raspberry!"

Plum gave Cherry her gift. "A fancy guitar case!" exclaimed Cherry.

"A new sewing kit!" said Raspberry when she opened Orange's gift. Then Lemon gave Orange some glittery hair clips, and the girls danced to the special song that Cherry had written for Lemon.

Finally, Strawberry and Blueberry opened their gifts. But when they saw what was in the packages, they both looked sad.

"What's wrong?" Cherry asked, noticing their sad faces.

"Blueberry, I traded my charm bracelet for your journal!" Strawberry confessed. "I wanted to give you a great gift to make you happy!"

"And I traded my favorite pen for your present!" Blueberry told Strawberry. "I thought that if I got you the charm, you'd know how much I care about you!"

"Blueberry, I don't need a fancy gift to show me how much you care!"
exclaimed Strawberry.

"And, Strawberry, your friendship is what makes me happy," said Blueberry.
"In fact, spending the holidays with all my friends is the best gift I can think of!"

"Wait!" said Orange. "There are a couple more presents to open!"
"More gifts?" asked Strawberry, confused.
Orange and Raspberry handed both Strawberry and Blueberry another present.
Inside the boxes were . . .

. . . Strawberry's bracelet and Blueberry's pen!

"We couldn't let you give away your favorite things!" said Orange.

"Thank you!" cried Strawberry and Blueberry together. "You are the best.
And this is the merriest Christmas ever!"

34

The Snow Dance

By Amy Ackelsberg
Illustrated by Laura Thomas

One winter morning, Strawberry Shortcake woke up to find
Berry Bitty City under a blanket of fluffy, white snow.
"How berry beautiful!" Strawberry cried. "I'm going to invite
all my friends out to play."

Soon, Strawberry and her friends were bundled up in their warmest clothes and outside enjoying the snow.

Raspberry Torte and Lemon Meringue built a snowman.

Orange Blossom and Blueberry Muffin zipped down the hill on their sled.

Strawberry and Plum Pudding made snow angels.

39

Strawberry pointed at the snow angels. "It looks just like they're dancing!" she said.

Then Strawberry glanced at the frozen lake. "I have a fruitastic idea!" she exclaimed. "Let's put on an ice-skating show to celebrate winter!"

40

"What a great idea!" agreed Lemon.

"We can invite everyone in Berry Bitty City!" said Raspberry.

"Come on," said Strawberry. "We can warm up and plan the show at my café."

As the girls sipped hot chocolate, they talked about the show. "Since Strawberry is such a great planner, she should be the director," Orange suggested.
Everyone agreed that this was a berry good idea!

Then each girl volunteered her help. Raspberry would make the costumes. Lemon would do hair and makeup. Blueberry would make the programs. And Orange would build the sets.

"And since Plum is the berry best dancer," said Strawberry, "she should be the star of the show!"

Plum spent the next afternoon teaching all her friends the dance. It was filled with lots of twirls and whirls!

44

"How beautiful," they all cried.
"Thank you," said Plum. "I call it the Snow Dance."

Over the next few days, Raspberry sewed costumes out of sparkly fabric.

Blueberry designed amazing programs.

46

Orange built a fantastic set.
Strawberry put up signs about the show.

The day before the show, the girls held one last practice on the ice.

They spun and jumped and danced and dipped.

"Berry good!" cried Strawberry.

48

Next, Plum practiced her solo.
She did a leap and a graceful glide,
but during her final spin . . .

. . . Plum fell on the ice!

"Oh no!" gasped Blueberry. "Are you all right?"

"I'll be okay," Plum replied. "But I can't skate in the show tomorrow."

"What will we do?" cried Lemon.

"Hmmm," said Orange. "I have an idea!"

Orange went home and worked late into the night.

The next morning, Orange asked Plum and Strawberry to come
to her store. She had a surprise for them.
    "I came up with a way for Plum to still be in the show!" said Orange.
"She can sit in this sled while the Berrykins pull her across the ice!"

"You are the berry best!" Plum told Orange.
"The show is saved!" cried Strawberry.

Now it was time for the girls to get ready for the Snow Dance.
At Lemon's salon, Raspberry handed her friends their shimmery costumes.

Then Lemon did their hair and gave them all glittery makeup.

As everyone in Berry Bitty City settled into their seats, Strawberry, Orange, Lemon, Blueberry, and Raspberry took their places on the ice.

The music started and the girls swooped and swished and whirled and twirled. Their moves were perfect!

When Strawberry gave a special signal, the Berrykins pulled the sled onto the ice. Plum sat inside, smiling and waving to the crowd.

The audience clapped and whistled.

"Plum, you were the star of the show!" Strawberry said as she handed Plum a bunch of roses.

"Thanks. But it couldn't have happened without all of you," Plum replied. Then she gave a rose to each of her best friends. "We make the berry best team!"

My First Sleepover

By Lauren Cecil
Illustrated by Terry Workman

One afternoon, Strawberry Shortcake was shopping
at Raspberry Torte's store.

As Strawberry was looking through the pajamas, she got a great idea.
"We should have a sleepover party!" Strawberry said excitedly.

"A sleepover?" asked Raspberry. She didn't sound as excited as Strawberry.
"Yes! It'll be berry fun," said Strawberry. "We can invite all our friends."

The next day, all the girls went to Strawberry's café to plan the sleepover party.

"We can have the party at my bookstore," said Blueberry Muffin.

"I'll bring music," said Plum Pudding.

"I can bring a movie," said Orange Blossom.
"I can bring stuff for makeovers," said Lemon Meringue.
"And I can bring snacks!" added Strawberry.

"Raspberry, what do you want to bring?" Strawberry asked.

"I'm really busy at my store," said Raspberry. "I don't think I have time to help."

"That's okay," said Strawberry. "All you need to bring is yourself!"

The day before the party, Strawberry's phone rang.
"I'm not feeling well," Raspberry said. "I don't think
I can come to the sleepover."

Strawberry was worried. She and all her friends went to see Raspberry.
"Are you all right?" Strawberry asked.
"Every time we talk about the sleepover, my stomach feels all funny and my head gets dizzy," admitted Raspberry.

"Hmmm," said Blueberry. "Have you ever been to a sleepover?"

"Never," answered Raspberry shyly.

"Maybe you feel sick because you're nervous about doing something new," Orange said.

"Maybe you're right," said Raspberry. "I don't know if I will like sleepovers. What if I get homesick?"

"Bring your favorite stuffed animal with you," said Orange. "It will remind you of home."

"What if I wake up in the middle of the night?" Raspberry asked.
"Think of your favorite story until you fall back asleep," Plum said.

"And if those things don't work, you can go home whenever you want," Strawberry said.

"Okay," Raspberry agreed. "I'll give sleepovers a try."

On the day of the party, Raspberry packed up her things and went to Blueberry's bookstore. She was still a little nervous.

"Hi, Raspberry!" Blueberry said. "I'm so glad you're here. We're going to have lots of fun!"

First, the girls danced to their favorite songs.
Raspberry loved bopping to the beat!

Then the girls snacked on Strawberry's triple-berry muffins.
Yum, thought Raspberry. *Strawberry's muffins are berry-licious!*

After that, the girls gave one another makeovers.

Raspberry giggled when she saw her new look!

At the end of the night, the girls curled up and watched a movie.

When the movie was over, Strawberry asked, "Raspberry, are you having fun?"
But Raspberry didn't answer. She was already asleep!

In the morning, the girls went to Strawberry's café for breakfast. As they ate, Strawberry asked Raspberry, "What did you think of your first sleepover?"

"It was great," Raspberry answered. "But there was one problem . . ."
"Oh no!" Strawberry gasped. "What went wrong?"

"It was over too soon!" said Raspberry. "I had so
much fun! I can't wait until we do it again!"

Meet Cherry Jam!

By Amy Ackelsberg
Illustrated by Laura Thomas

Strawberry Shortcake and her friends were berry excited. Their favorite superstar, Cherry Jam, was moving to Berry Bitty City!

"I can't wait to meet Cherry Jam!" cried Lemon Meringue.
"I know all her songs by heart!" exclaimed Plum Pudding.
"She's berry talented!" Raspberry Torte added.

86

"I have an idea," said Strawberry. "Let's have a party
at my café to welcome Cherry!"
"Yes!" said Orange Blossom and Blueberry Muffin.

Strawberry and her friends spent the next day getting ready for the party.

They put up decorations and baked tasty treats.

At the party that night, the café was crowded.
Everyone in Berry Bitty City wanted to meet Cherry Jam!

When Cherry arrived, Strawberry and her friends introduced themselves.
"It's berry nice to meet you!" Strawberry told Cherry.
"We can't wait to hang out with you!" exclaimed Plum.

"How sweet of you!" Cherry replied.
"Is it fun to be so famous?" Orange asked Cherry.
"Do you love wearing all the costumes and makeup?" added Lemon.

"Actually," said Cherry, "I'm taking some time off from the spotlight."
"But why?" cried Raspberry.
"Sometimes being famous can be berry lonely," Cherry explained. "I have lots of fans, but no true friends. I feel like no one knows the real me!"

"Hmm . . . ," said Strawberry. "I think we know just how to make you feel at home here in Berry Bitty City."

Over the next few days, Strawberry and her friends
took turns getting to know Cherry.
Raspberry and Cherry traded fashion advice. They designed
some outfits for Cherry's new life out of the spotlight.

Cherry visited Lemon's hair salon. Lemon gave her a fabulous new look that was very different from the one Cherry wore when she was performing.

Blueberry and Cherry shared fruit smoothies at Blueberry's bookstore. They talked about their favorite books and movies.

Cherry went to Orange's store, where Orange helped Cherry shop for decorations for her new home.

At Plum's studio, Plum and Cherry worked on their dance moves.

Finally, Strawberry and Cherry wrote and rehearsed a few new songs.
"Let's invite our friends over to hear us perform," said Strawberry when
they were finished.
"Great idea!" Cherry agreed.

Soon all the girls were rocking to the rhythms of Cherry and Strawberry's new tunes.

Orange, Plum, and Raspberry grabbed instruments and joined in,
while Lemon and Blueberry bopped to the beat.

"That was berry good!" exclaimed Cherry when they took a break.
"We sound fruitastic!" Orange said.

"And we owe it all to you, Cherry," said Raspberry.
"Now that we know the real you!"
"You mean it?" asked Cherry shyly.

"Yes!" said Strawberry. "You're a talented singer who's supersweet and berry fun to be with."

"An all-around fabulous friend!" added Blueberry.

"Thank you," said Cherry. "And I think that not only have
I found the perfect pals . . ."

"I've found the perfect bandmates, too!" said Cherry.
"Yes!" exclaimed all of Cherry's new berry best friends.

Gymnastics Fun

By Mickie Matheis

Illustrated by Laura Thomas

One morning at the Berry Café, Strawberry Shortcake and her friends were about to eat some tasty strawberry-topped waffles when Plum Pudding burst through the front door.

"Girls . . . so excited . . . I can't . . . never believe . . . whoa!" she said breathlessly. She put her hand to her chest and dropped into a chair.

The girls laughed at their friend's enthusiasm. "Why are you so berry excited?" asked Strawberry.

Plum explained that a gymnastics coach named Misty Flutterbug had visited her at her dance studio earlier. Coach Misty had been a famous gymnast. Years ago, she won three gold medals in the Berry Big City Games.

"She wants to use my dance studio for a two-week gymnastics camp," Plum said. "I hope you'll sign up with me!"

The other girls agreed that gymnastics sounded like a lot of fun. They couldn't wait to begin!

111

The next day the girls gathered at Sweet Beats Studio for the first day of gymnastics camp. They wore their hair in ponytails and dressed in cute, colorful leotards.

112

Coach Misty told the girls more about the sport. She said good gymnasts were strong, flexible, and graceful.

So are dancers, Plum thought. *I'll bet this means I'll be good at gymnastics.*

"But the most important quality is having the courage to try new things," the coach finished.

Coach Misty began the class with some warm-up exercises.
First they ran a few laps. Then they did shoulder rolls and wrist
circles. Next they did leg and arm stretches. Finally they did splits
and bridges. Now they were ready to begin learning skills on
the equipment!

114

They started with the uneven bars. Coach Misty explained how to swing on the top bar. "I'll spot you," she told them. "Spotting means that I'll stand here and assist you in learning the skill."

She helped them while they practiced swinging on the bars.
After just a few tries, Strawberry and Raspberry Torte were both
able to swing on their own.

"Berry good!" said the coach. "Who would like to try next?"

Plum stepped forward. "I would!" she said eagerly.

Plum gave it a few tries, but she wasn't able to keep swinging by herself. She needed Coach Misty's help each time.

"You'll learn to do it on your own soon enough," the coach kindly told Plum.

The balance beam came next. Lemon Meringue and Cherry Jam climbed up onto it. The coach instructed them how to hold their arms out and walk. The girls moved smoothly to the end of the beam. They grinned and bowed before hopping off.

"Nicely done," Coach Misty said.

"Can I go?" asked Plum. She jumped up onto the beam, wobbled, and fell off the other side. She tried a second time, only to fall again.

The third time she got on, Coach Misty held Plum's hand and helped her walk across. "There you go! You can do it," she said. But Plum looked upset as she jumped down.

"Let's move on to the vault," suggested Coach Misty. The girls were thrilled when the former gymnast demonstrated a beautiful vault with a double twist. "Someday you'll learn to do that," she said as the girls clapped.

Orange Blossom and Blueberry Muffin volunteered to try the vault. The coach spotted the girls as they tried front handsprings. "Excellent!" she exclaimed as Orange and Blueberry performed them perfectly.

"My turn!" said Plum. She ran fast and hit the springboard hard. Unfortunately, she landed in a sitting position on the mat.

"I'm sure next time you'll stick your landing," said Coach Misty. "That's what we call it when we land on our feet."

Even though the coach was encouraging, Plum was disappointed with her performance. She got up and walked away. Her friends exchanged worried looks as Strawberry hurried after her.

Strawberry found Plum leaning against the ballet barre in one of the dance rooms. Plum was looking at herself in the long mirror. Her face was very sad.

"Plum, what's wrong?" asked Strawberry.

"I thought I would be good at gymnastics since I'm a dancer," confessed Plum. "But it's not easy—at least not for me."

"Remember what Coach Misty said?" Strawberry said gently. "You need to have the courage to try new things. You're the best dancer in Berry Bitty City because you work hard to learn different moves and then practice them until they're perfect."

"You're right, Strawberry. Just because gymnastics is harder than I expected doesn't mean I should give up so easily. I'll go back out and try again," Plum said.

When the girls got back, Coach Misty was teaching everyone a simple floor routine. "Would you like to go first?" She smiled at Plum.

Plum nodded and took her place on the floor.

Everyone watched as she performed the routine
exactly as the coach had. Plum even added her own
touch at the end—a lovely arabesque.

Plum's friends ran over and surrounded her with
hugs. "That was beautiful! We knew you could do it!"
they all cheered at the same time.

"See how much fun it can be to try new things?" Strawberry said.

"Yes!" Plum replied. "And it's even better when I try them with my berry best friends."

A Berry Bitty
Ballet

By Amy Ackelsberg
Illustrated by Laura Thomas

One morning, Strawberry Shortcake went to visit her friend Plum Pudding at her ballet studio. When she got there, Plum was hanging a poster for a new ballet coming to Berry Bitty City.

"We should try out with all our friends!" exclaimed Strawberry.

"Great idea!" said Plum.

On the day of the auditions, Strawberry and her friends joined the line of townspeople waiting to try out.

"This is berry exciting!" exclaimed Orange Blossom and Blueberry Muffin.
"I can't wait to get onstage!" said Plum.
"Me neither!" cried Strawberry.
"Let's get warmed up!" said Cherry Jam as she began to lead the
girls in some stretches.

One by one, the girls performed. They leaped and twirled and pirouetted.

Then Postmaster Bumblebee, Sadiebug, and Mr. Longface Caterpillar tried out, too.

When the results were posted . . .

. . . all the girls got parts!

"We're going to be butterflies!" exclaimed Orange and Plum.

"We're going to be dancing flowers!" said Lemon Meringue, Raspberry Torte, and Blueberry.

"Cherry, you won the lead role!" cried Strawberry.

"And, Strawberry, you're my understudy!" said Cherry. "That means we'll work together!"

"Great!" exclaimed Strawberry. "Let's go learn our parts and start rehearsing!"

The girls practiced every day to prepare for the big performance.
Orange and Plum learned to flutter their arms like graceful butterflies.
Raspberry, Lemon, and Blueberry danced and swayed like beautiful flowers
blowing in the wind.

"This is so much fun!" exclaimed Strawberry as she and Cherry took turns spinning and jumping. Then they linked arms and did a final curtsy.
"Fruitastic!" cried their friends.

Soon it was the day of the big dress rehearsal.
"Time to try on our costumes!" said Raspberry.
There were glittery butterfly wings for Orange and Plum and colorful fabric
flowers for Raspberry, Blueberry, and Lemon.

There was a beautiful pink tutu for Cherry, but there was nothing for Strawberry.

"I'm sorry, Strawberry," said Cherry. "You'll wear my costume if I can't perform in the show."

"Okay," said Strawberry sadly. Then she sat and watched while her friends danced under the spotlight.

The next day, Strawberry was at the café having lunch
with Blueberry and Orange.
"I can't wait for the show!" said Blueberry.
"Me neither!" agreed Orange. "What about you, Strawberry?"

144

"Well," said Strawberry, "I know the understudy is an important job, but I wish I could be in the ballet, too!" Suddenly, Strawberry's phone rang . . .

"We need you, Strawberry!" said Berrykin Bloom. "Cherry is sick! She can't perform in the ballet!"

"Oh no!" cried Strawberry. "Poor Cherry!"

Strawberry hurried to Plum's studio, where Plum helped her practice until her moves were perfect. Raspberry made sure Strawberry's tutu fit just right, and Lemon gave her a special hairstyle.

On the night of the performance, the theater was crowded with townspeople. They took their seats as the lights dimmed. The curtain lifted and the ballet began!

148

The dancers whirled and twirled and the audience clapped and cheered.
"Bravo!" they shouted.
Strawberry and her friends took a big bow.

"Great job, Strawberry!" Plum said after the curtain had closed. "You really saved the day!"

"Thanks, Plum," replied Strawberry. "I'm happy that I got a chance to perform, but now I'm sad that Cherry couldn't be here!"

"I have an idea!" said Orange. "Let's go visit Cherry and tell her about the show!"

"Yes!" cried her friends.

But when they walked backstage, they found . . .

"Cherry!" exclaimed Lemon. "Are you feeling better?"

"I wasn't sick," Cherry confessed. "I was only pretending, so that Strawberry could dance in the ballet."

"Oh, Cherry, you didn't have to do that!" cried Strawberry.
"I know," Cherry replied. "But I could tell how much you
wanted to be in the show!"

Strawberry gave Cherry a big hug.

"Cherry, I'm so lucky to have a berry best friend like you!" said Strawberry.

"Thank you, Strawberry," said Cherry. "I'd trade the spotlight for your friendship any day."

BERRY CUTE!

LET IT SNOW

I ♥ Strawberry!

Friends Forever

To:

_____

From:

To:

_____

From:

To:

_____

From:

To:

_____

From: